GREEK GODS

#squadgoals

⚡

MORE OMG CLASSICS!

srsly Hamlet

YOLO Juliet

Macbeth #killingit

A Midsummer Night #nofilter

Darcy Swipes Left

Scrooge #worstgiftever

GREEK GODS
#squadgoals

courtney carbone

Random House 🏛 New York

To Mom and Dad, thanks for not eating me. 🍴
—C.B.C.

Text copyright © 2017 by Penguin Random House LLC
Emoji copyright © Apple Inc.
Images on page 1, earth © Shutterstock/NPeter, sky © Shutterstock/Thaiview;
page 9 © Shutterstock/GagliardiImages; page 25 © Shutterstock/IMG Stock Studio;
page 35 © Shutterstock/krungchingpixs; page 39 © Shutterstock/Matt Gibson;
page 46 © Shutterstock/mariocigic; page 60 © Shutterstock/Santia; page 78
© Shutterstock/Nastya Nikitina; page 84 © Shutterstock/Slawomir Fajer; page 105
© Shutterstock/Amitry Sheremeta; page 110 © Shutterstock/EpicStockMedia

Visit us on the Web! randomhouseteens.com

Educators and librarians, for a variety of teaching tools,
visit us at RHTeachersLibrarians.com

Library of Congress Cataloging-in-Publication Data is available upon request.
ISBN 978-1-5247-1564-9 (trade) — ISBN 978-1-5247-1565-6 (ebook)

MANUFACTURED IN CHINA

10 9 8 7 6 5 4 3 2 1

First Edition

who's who

Gaia: Mother Earth

Uranus: Father Sky

Zeus: King of the Gods

Hera: Goddess of Marriage, Women, Childbirth, and Family

Ares: God of War

Hephaestus: God of Fire

Aphrodite: Goddess of Love and Beauty

Hermes: Herald of the Gods

Demeter: Goddess of the Harvest

Persephone: Goddess of Springtime

Poseidon: God of the Sea

Athena: Goddess of Wisdom

Hestia: Goddess of the Hearth

Apollo: God of Music and Light

Artemis: Goddess of the Hunt

Dionysus: God of Wine

Hades: God of the Underworld

Leto: Goddess of Motherhood

Eros: God of Attraction and Desire

Medusa: Gorgon

Perseus: Gorgon Slayer

who's who (cont.)

👁 **Brontes:** Cyclops

👁 **Steropes:** Cyclops

👁 **Arges:** Cyclops

🙌 **Briares:** Hekatonkheir

🙌 **Kottos:** Hekatonkheir

🙌 **Gyes:** Hekatonkheir

💪 **Theia:** Titaness

💪 **Rhea:** Titaness

💪 **Themis:** Titaness

💪 **Mnemosyne:** Titaness

💪 **Phoebe:** Titaness

💪 **Tethys:** Titaness

💪 **Oceanus:** Titan

💪 **Hyperion:** Titan

💪 **Koios:** Titan

💪 **Krios:** Titan

💪 **Iapetus:** Titan

💪 **Kronos:** Titan

🧔 **Atlas:** Titan

👸 **Metis:** wife and cousin of Zeus

Send

Prometheus: creator of mankind (somehow)

Actaeon: son of a herdsman

Orion: hunter and, later, a constellation

Echo: nymph

Narcissus: hunter

Oracle of Delphi: priestess with powers of prophecy

Tantalus: very, very bad father

Pelops: King of Pisa and creator of the Olympic games

Niobe: not important

Hippodamia: Princess and, later, Queen of Pisa

Icarus: some dumb kid

Daedalus: master craftsman

King of Chios: king

Princess of Chios: princess

King Midas: king

Princess Marigold: princess

King Minos: king

King of Sicily: king

King Oenomaus: king

Oedipus: king and tragic hero

Queen Jocasta: queen

King Laius: king

Otis: giant twin

Ephialtes: giant twin

Send

- Gaia and Uranus -

Gaia

Does this pic make me look round?

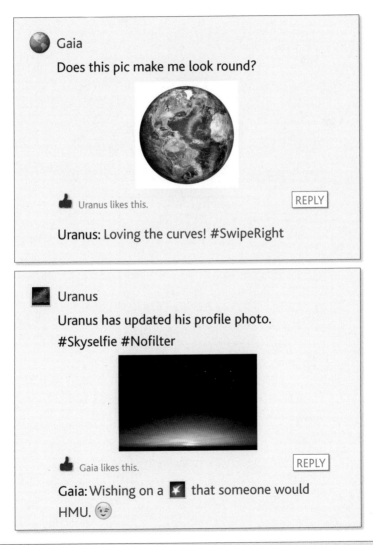

👍 Uranus likes this.

REPLY

Uranus: Loving the curves! #SwipeRight

Uranus

Uranus has updated his profile photo.
#Skyselfie #Nofilter

👍 Gaia likes this.

REPLY

Gaia: Wishing on a ⭐ that someone would HMU. 😉

Send

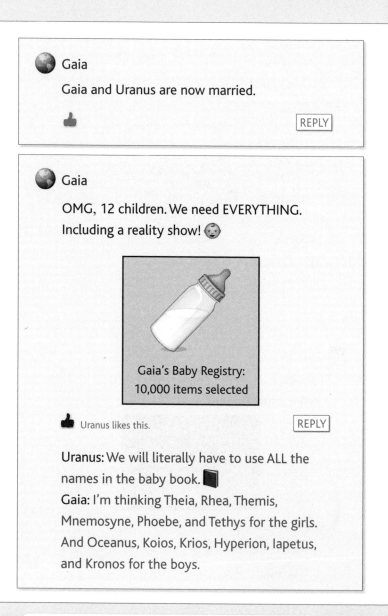

Gaia

Gaia and Uranus are now married.

👍 REPLY

Gaia

OMG, 12 children. We need EVERYTHING.
Including a reality show! 👶

Gaia's Baby Registry:
10,000 items selected

👍 Uranus likes this. REPLY

Uranus: We will literally have to use ALL the
names in the baby book. 📖
Gaia: I'm thinking Theia, Rhea, Themis,
Mnemosyne, Phoebe, and Tethys for the girls.
And Oceanus, Koios, Krios, Hyperion, Iapetus,
and Kronos for the boys.

Send

Uranus: Ok. What will we call the boys as a group? Something MANLY.

Gaia: How about the Titans?

Uranus: I can live with that. And we can call the girls the Titanettes! No, the Titanelles! No, the Titanesses! Yeah.

Gaia: Titanesses. Really?

Uranus: Impossible to make fun of. Like Uranus.

Gaia: Lol, yeah. Hopefully they grow up to be exactly like you. 🙄

Uranus: Well, not exactly like me. If they become 2 strong, I'll have to kill them, LOL. 💪

🌍 Gaia

Three more babies! 🍼🍼🍼 Brontes, Steropes, and Arges. We'll call them the Cyclopes.

👍   REPLY

Uranus: What's up with these 3? Something looks off. Not sure what, tho. . . . 🤔

Send

Gaia: Srsly?

Uranus: Don't tell me—is it their hair color???

Gaia: They each have only 1 eye in the middle of their forehead. 👁

Uranus: BABE, I TOLD YOU NOT TO TELL ME! But yeah, that's totally it. What did I name them again?

Gaia: Lightning, Thunder, and Thunderbolt.

Uranus: Lol, yeah, I think I was a little drunk when I came up with the 3rd one. 🍺 But it's OK. I hate them. LOL

Leto's Baby Emporium

Coats: 3
Hats: 150
Mittens: 300

Total: $4,304 drachmas

****

Send

uranus

Babe. Why does the receipt say you bought 3 coats, 150 hats, and 300 mittens?

Gaia

I just gave birth again.

uranus

I thought that was water weight?!

Gaia

Sigh. 70% of my surface is water. I had 3 babies. We're going to call them the Hekatonkheires. Their names are Briares, Kottos, and Gyes.

uranus

UGH. That's going to remind me of Gyes from work. You know I hate that guy.

Gaia

I gave birth to EIGHTEEN babies. You will deal with a name you don't like.

Send

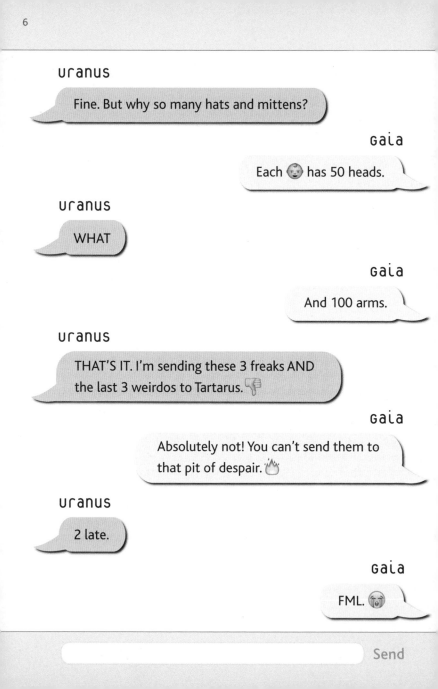

Group text: Gaia, Oceanus, Hyperion, Koios, Krios, Iapetus, Kronos

Gaia

Titans, listen up. Your dad is driving me nuts. 🌀 Can 1 of u pls kill him? 😵 THX. Love you!

Oceanus

Not it. 🗳️

Hyperion

Not it. 🚴

Koios

Not it. 🏇

Krios

Not it. 🏂

Iapetus

Not it. 🏄

Kronos

Ugh. Fine, I'll do it. But u guys owe me! 🏋️

Send

Kronos

Guess there's a new 👑 in town. KRONOS
FTW. #RIPUranus #OverthrowBackThursday

👍 Gaia likes this.   REPLY

Group text: Cyclopes, Hekatonkheires, Kronos

cyclopes

Kronos, can u pls free us from Tartarus now? 🔥

Hekatonkheires

Yeah, and us too? 🔥 🔥

Kronos

Not rite now. Busy. 🍹 ☀️ 🏖️

Send

- Kronos and Rhea -

Kronos

Kronos and Rhea are now married.

REPLY

Rhea

It's a boy! #Zeus

Kronos

Nom nom nom 😋

Rhea

STOP EATING ALL OUR KIDS 🍴 #RIPHestia #RIPHades #RIPDemeter #RIPHera #RIPPoseidon

Kronos

Can't help it. Gotta make sure they don't get strong enough 2 kill me. #DaddyIssues

Send

Kronos

Also, they are delicious + free. 😜

💪 Mnemosyne

Mnemosyne, Tethys, Theia, Phoebe, and Themis were tagged in the album: Happy, Normal Families with Fathers Who Don't Eat Their Kids.

👍   REPLY

Rhea: Show-offs 😠

Mnemosyne: Hey! It's not our fault u married a guy w/ an insatiable appetite for his own offspring!

Rhea: Do u think I would have 💒 him if I knew he'd eat our kids?!?!

Themis: IDK. Who knows wut u r into? 😏

👍 Kronos likes this.

Kronos

Hey, bae, did u give birth 2 that new kid yet?

Rhea

Yes. His name is Zeus. ⚡

Send

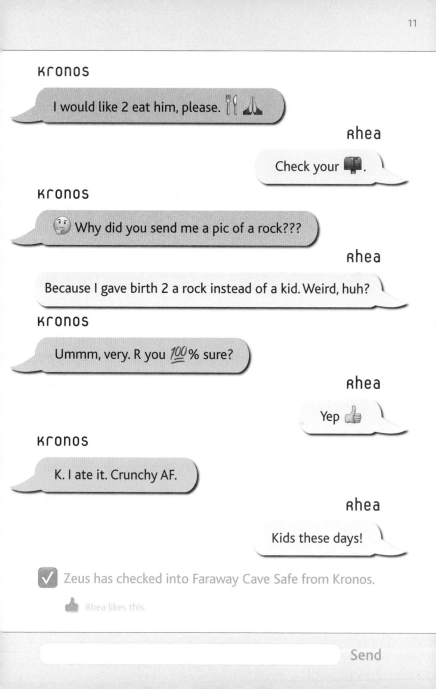

- Zeus, the Titans, and Every1 Else -

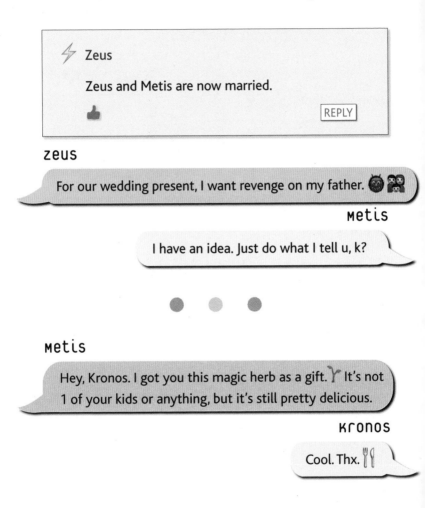

💪 **Kronos**

That magic herb made me so 🤮 I just threw up ALL my kids, including that one who looked like a rock! ROTFLMAO 😂

👍 Hades, Poseidon, Hestia, Demeter, Hera, and Rock like this.

REPLY

Hades: The inside of your stomach was terrifying. 💀 And keep in mind I'm the god of the underworld. SMH.

💀 **Hades**

Hades, Poseidon, Hestia, Demeter, Hera, and Zeus have created a group: Time to Get Revenge on Dad for Eating Us.

👍

REPLY

Kronos: Yikes. Ummm. Hi, kids. 😅 I g2g. 👋 Zeus is in charge.

Send

Group text: Oceanus, Hyperion, Koios, Krios, Iapetus

oceanus

> Did you guys see wut just happened? ICYMI, Dad gave all his power 2 our younger siblings. WTF. #FirstBorns

Hyperion

> We should be in charge. 💪

koios

> Agreed! 😠

krios

> 🤔 What should we do?

iapetus

> Let's take them ⬇️!

● ● ●

zeus

> Hey, Mom, whatever happened 2 those weird brothers & sisters we used 2 have? #Cyclopes #Hekatonkheires

Send

Gaia

They are in 🔥 Tartarus 🔥 bc ur father couldn't stand 2 look @ them.

Zeus

Tartarus. U mean that sauce Poseidon puts on his sandwiches? I always thought it tasted funny. 🐟🐠🐡🐟🦐

Gaia

No, it's a PLACE. I'll send u the address.

Zeus

K, cool. I'm going to free them. #FreeTartarus

✅ Zeus has checked into Tartarus.

 Cyclopes and Hekatonkheires like this.

Send

Poseidon

Check out this bad@$$ trident my long-lost siblings made me! 🎁

👍 REPLY

⚡ Zeus

Zeus has ordered a T-shirt: I went to Tartarus to free my siblings, and all I got were these lousy lightning bolts. ⚡ ⚡

👍 REPLY

Hades: Zeus is lit!
Hera: 😂

Send

💀 Hades

And check out my Invisibility Helmet.

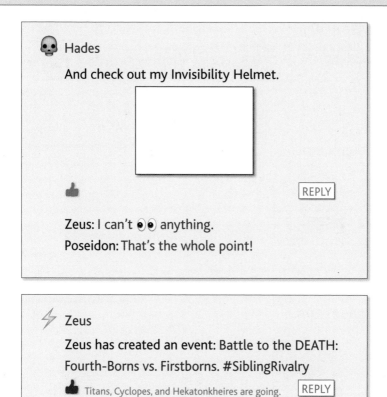

👍   REPLY

Zeus: I can't 👀 anything.
Poseidon: That's the whole point!

⚡ Zeus

Zeus has created an event: Battle to the DEATH: Fourth-Borns vs. Firstborns. #SiblingRivalry

👍 Titans, Cyclopes, and Hekatonkheires are going.   REPLY

Poseidon: Is this a land thing? Ugh. Why is everything always on LAND???

Send ·

⚡ **Zeus**

We won! Way 2 go, Fourth-Borns! Titans, you are 4ever banished to Tartarus. And, Hekatonkheires, I want u 2 stay there & guard them.

👍 | REPLY |

Atlas: Wasn't the whole point of this 2 free ur siblings from Tartarus? 🔥

Zeus: That's enough out of you, person I'm related to but not sure how. Go hold this super-heavy sky thing 4ever on ur shoulders.

Atlas: You mean that globe?

Zeus: It's not a globe! ❌ 🌑 It's the heavens!!

Atlas: It looks like a globe. 🌑 Ppl are going 2 think it's a globe. 🌑

Zeus: That's ENOUGH. 😠 Just do as I say.

Atlas: Fine. But don't say I didn't warn u. . . .

ɪapetus

Son, check it out. You're trending! #FreeAtlas

Atlas

Shrugs NBD.

Send

- Athena and Zeus -

Congratulations!

You have been randomly selected
to receive one free prediction
from Daily Oracle!

CLICK HERE

From: Daily Oracle
To: Zeus
Subject: I predict that . . .

You will open this email!
Want to see more 100% accurate predictions?
Subscribe now to lock in rock-bottom prices!

Free prediction for member "Zeus":

Your wife will have a
son who will overthrow you.

Send

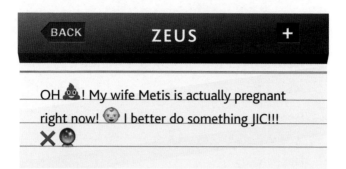

OH 💩! My wife Metis is actually pregnant right now! 👶 I better do something JIC!!! ✖️🔮

Zeus To-Do List

3 items   Edit

☑ Swallow Metis and unborn child whole

☑ Hit on all the ladies

☐ Polish lightning bolts

Send

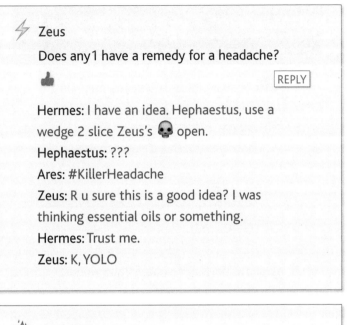

⚡ **Zeus**

Does any1 have a remedy for a headache?

👍   REPLY

Hermes: I have an idea. Hephaestus, use a wedge 2 slice Zeus's 💀 open.
Hephaestus: ???
Ares: #KillerHeadache
Zeus: R u sure this is a good idea? I was thinking essential oils or something.
Hermes: Trust me.
Zeus: K, YOLO

🔥 **Hephaestus**

Whoa! So weird. As soon as I chopped open Zeus's 💀, a fully formed human dressed in armor sprang out! #EnterAthena #BrainChild

👍 Athena likes this.   REPLY

Send

- Gods of Mount Olympus -

 The Cyclopes have checked into Towering Palace on Top of Mount Olympus.

 Cyclopes and Hekatonkheires like this.

⚡ **Zeus**

Zeus has created a quiz: "Which god or goddess are you? Post ur answers below."

👍 REPLY

Ares: God of War ⚔️

Hephaestus: God of Fire 🔥

Aphrodite: Goddess of Love & Beauty 💟

Hermes: I got Herald of the Gods. Lame!
I wanted Supreme Joker. Ares, want to trade? 🃏

Ares: Sure.

Hermes: Rly??

Ares: No way, dude! Ur title sux.

Demeter: Goddess of the Harvest 🌾

Poseidon: God of the Sea 🌊

Athena: Goddess of Wisdom ⚖️

Apollo: God of Music & Light 🎼 . . . & amateur live performances 🎤🎵

Send

Artemis: Goddess of the Hunt 🏹
Dionysus: godof win
Dionysus: godd f w1ne
Dionysus: 🍷
Hades: God of the Underworld!!! 💀
Athena: Typical Hades. Always a downer.

⚡ Zeus

Zeus and Hera have posted 25 new pictures to the album: Wedding of the Year.

👍 Aphrodite likes this.

REPLY

Hermes: #IncestLaVie

Plenty of Gods

Message Me

Send Me a Gift

ZeusOnTheLoose

Looking for: **Anyone other than my wife**

First name: **Zeus**

Gender: **Male**

Wanted: **No relationship or commitment of any kind**

Location: **Mount Olympus**

Profession: **God**

Religion: **Myself**

Ethnicity: **Greek**

Do you have children? **Yes**

Body type: **Prefer not to say**

Sign: ⚡ **Thunderbolt** ⚡

Hera

U left a dating app open on ur phone this a.m.!!!
I still can't believe u tricked me into marrying u. 😠

Send

zeus

Yeah. Pretending to b a defenseless little bird and letting you fall in 🖤 w/ me was legit the #BestIdeaEver #ZeusFTW

нега

Send

- Aphrodite -

Aphrodite
Kind of having an identity crisis here. No one knows where I came from. Ppl keep saying I was born out of sea foam—or worse. WTF 🌊

👍
REPLY

Zeus
Zeus has created an event: Aphrodite's Wedding to Hephaestus.

👍 Zeus likes this.
REPLY

Aphrodite: Srsly, Dad? The blacksmith? FML

● ● ●

Group text: Aphrodite, Hephaestus, Eros

Aphrodite

Hephaestus! Have u 👂 what our son has been doing?

Hephaestus

Sigh Eros, have u been shooting people w/ 🏹s again? 🏹

Send

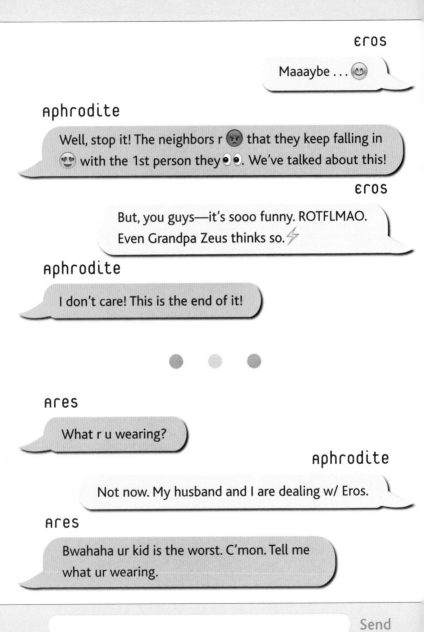

Aphrodite

Fine. My gold girdle w/ all the magic filigree.

Ares

OMG u look so hot in that. 🔥🔥🔥

Aphrodite

Hephaestus made it for me. ⚒️ Besides, I look hot in everything. 💋

Ares

IDK why the 😈 ur still w/ that guy. He's such a loser.

Aphrodite

It's not like I wanted 2 💒 him! Zeus made me. But I feel bad bc he's so nice. Like literally, THE nicest guy. And you're kind of a 💩head TBH.

Ares

Well, you don't become the #GodOfWar by holding 🚪s and helping little 👵s cross the street.

Aphrodite

Lolz. Ur just lucky ur hot. I'll 👀 u later. 😘

- Leto and Niobe -

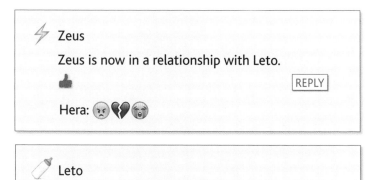

⚡ **Zeus**

Zeus is now in a relationship with Leto.

👍   REPLY

Hera: 😡 💔 😭

🍼 **Leto**

Leto has registered for "His and Hers Cribs" at Mount Olympus Baby: Where the Prices Are Heroic #Artemis #Apollo

👍   REPLY

Leto

> Hey. I am going 2 have the twins any day now. 📅
> Did u find somewhere safe 4 me to give birth? 🏔️

Zeus

> Well . . . Hera is jealous again, u being my new wife & all, and kinda forbade all the lands on 🌍 from letting u give birth. 😬 🙊 🙈

Send

Leto

WHAT?!?! I'm not going 2 do some kind of weird water birth, if that's what ur thinking.

zeus

Don't freak out—there is this 1 little island, Delos, that doesn't *technically* fall under her rule. 🏝️ 👍

Leto

Fine. What's there?

zeus

Leto

Yeah, what else?

zeus

Um, that's it. Delos is literally a tiny island with one palm tree. 🏝️

Leto

FML

Send

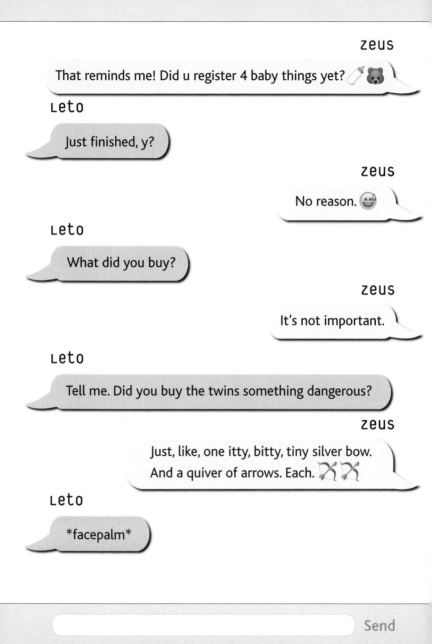

zeus

Before u lose it, 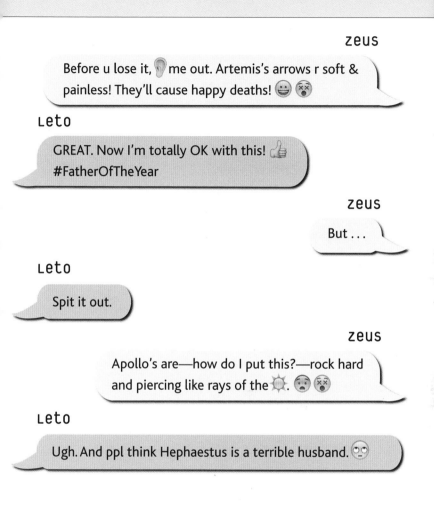 me out. Artemis's arrows r soft & painless! They'll cause happy deaths! 😀 😵

Leto

GREAT. Now I'm totally OK with this! 👍 #FatherOfTheYear

zeus

But . . .

Leto

Spit it out.

zeus

Apollo's are—how do I put this?—rock hard and piercing like rays of the ☀. 😨 😵

Leto

Ugh. And ppl think Hephaestus is a terrible husband. 🙄

Send

🍼 **Leto**

I love my kids SO much. 💚 Artemis & Apollo, u guys mean the 🌍 2 me! #ProudMama

👍

REPLY

Niobe: Oh, u only have 2 kids? That's so sad! 🥺 I have 14 kids. Family is so important to me. #Blessed

Apollo: You mean you HAD 7 sons before you posted that super obnoxious msg.

Artemis: And you HAD 7 daughters before you came @ my mom.

Leto: Guys, did u 2 just kill all of Niobe's kids?

Apollo: Mom, she was talking crap about u!!!

Artemis: What were we supposed 2 do?

Niobe: WAHHHHHHH 😭

Random Gods: Niobe, don't be 😔! We can help! We'll turn u into a rock so u don't feel feelings anymore! (But watch out 4 Kronos, cos he might try and eat u.)

Send

🧑 Niobe

Even as a rock, water flows from me like tears. 😭

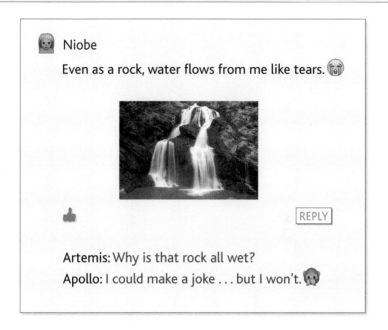

👍   REPLY

Artemis: Why is that rock all wet?

Apollo: I could make a joke . . . but I won't. 🙊

Send

- Artemis -

Artemis

Dad, can I talk 2 u about something?

Zeus

Of course! I'm not like those other dads.
I'm a cool dad! 😎 What's up?

Artemis

🙄 Ntm. But can you promise never to make me get married & settle down? 👰 ❌ I rly just want to hunt my whole life. 🏹 🐗 🐂 🐃 🐑

Zeus

You do you, honey. Fine w/ me. 👍

Artemis

There is this other thing. . . .

Zeus

?

Send

Artemis

Can I have 50 nymphs 2 keep me company?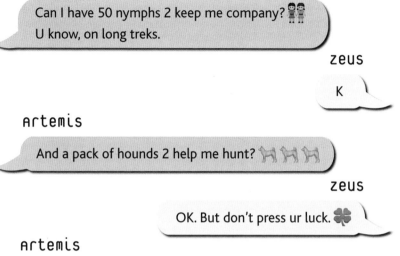
U know, on long treks.

zeus

K

Artemis

And a pack of hounds 2 help me hunt?

zeus

OK. But don't press ur luck.

Artemis

Thx!

Send

Artemis

Artemis has added "Bathing out in the open" to her interests.

👍 REPLY

Actaeon

Actaeon has added "Watching Artemis bathe out in the open" to his interests.

👍 REPLY

Artemis: R u serious, mortal? 😠

Actaeon: 😍 I can't help it! U r so beautiful.

Artemis: Don't make me throw this magical water on u so u turn into a stag. 🦌

Actaeon: LOL, ur so cute when ur 😠. 😘

Artemis: Don't say I didn't warn you. . . .

Send

Actaeon

Actaeon has updated his profile photo.

 Artemis likes this.

REPLY

Hermes: Now that's what I call going stag. 😂
Actaeon: Oh no! Wild beasts are coming right at me! I think they are going to kil

---

🏹 **Artemis**

Stupid mortals. You can't just stare @ ppl naked & expect nothing 2 happen!!! 🛁
Back 2 hunting. Let's go, nymphs. XO

👍

REPLY

Send

- Otis and Ephialtes -

Otis

Otis and Ephialtes have updated their profiles on GodBod. #BFF #BUFF

👍 Poseidon likes this.

REPLY

💪 GodBod 💪

Otis is now 99.9% muscle.

Ephialtes is now 99.9% muscle.

Group text: Poseidon, Otis, Ephialtes

poseidon

Did you guys just go through another growth spurt? You're almost as big as ur old man! 👴

otis

I'm about 60 feet now. NBD 💪

ephialtes

Same. But if we keep growing, no1 will want 2 date us. 🙁 💔

Send

poseidon

True. But no1 will want 2 overthrow u, either! 👍

otis

That's true, I guess. But I'm kind of into Artemis. 🏹

ephialtes

Yeah. She could overthrow me any day. 😉

<BACK   **GAIA**   +

Still pretty pissed @ Zeus 4 sending my kids to Tartarus . . . and can't help but notice how big Otis & Ephialtes have gotten. 💪🤔 I wonder if I could convince them 2 overthrow Zeus. . . . Here goes nothing! 🙀

Group text: Gaia, Otis, Ephialtes

Gaia

Hey, guys. Any chance u'd be interested in helping me take ⬇️ Zeus? ⚡

Send

otis

That's a great idea! 💡 Why don't we pile those 2  on top of each other and 👀 if we can make a sweet NEW  the size of Olympus?

ephialtes

YESSS! THAT!

gaia

✅ Otis and Ephialtes have checked into Enormous New Mountain to Rival Olympus.

👍 Gaia likes this.

Zeus: WTF?! Is this for real?
Ephialtes: Yep! #NoFilter
Zeus: NOT WHAT I MEANT
Otis: Check ur

Send

Group text: Ephialtes, Otis, Artemis, Hera, Zeus, Ares, Apollo

ephialtes

Surrender, Zeus! ⚡ We're going to rule the 🌍 now.

otis

Yeah! And also I want 2 💍 ur daughter Artemis. 👰🤵

ephialtes

Yeah, and I want 2 marry ur wife Hera. 😍

Artemis

facepalm

Hera

rolls eyes

zeus

R u sure that's what u want? R u sure u don't want ALL THESE FIERY THUNDERBOLTS HURLED AT YOUR FACE?! ⚡⚡⚡

Ares

A fight! HECK YES! I'm in. 👊

Send

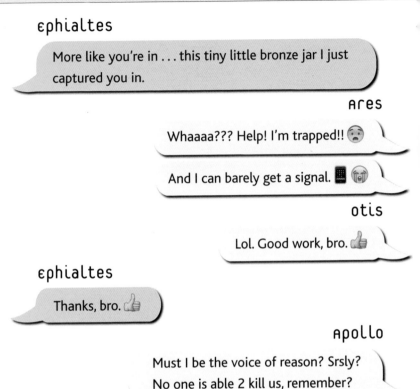

ephialtes

More like you're in . . . this tiny little bronze jar I just captured you in.

ares

Whaaaa??? Help! I'm trapped!! 😨

And I can barely get a signal. 📱 😭

otis

Lol. Good work, bro. 👍

ephialtes

Thanks, bro. 👍

apollo

Must I be the voice of reason? Srsly? No one is able 2 kill us, remember?

otis

Well, we'll find out soon enough, won't we?

apollo

I don't have ⏰ 4 this. Artemis, what do u think we should do? <wink, wink>

Send

artemis

Right. Uh, Otis, yes, I totally want 2 marry you. And I'm not just saying that bc it's part of a much larger plan.

otis

Whoa! And I thought this was going 2 b hard lol.

artemis

Yeah. Uh, I'm so in  w/ u even tho we just met via this awkward txt chain. Let's run away together 2 the 🏝 of Naxos. Which BTW is a random 🏝 I have chosen just now. Because romance. 👫

otis

Great! See u there. xo

ephialtes

So, Hera, do u have anything u want 2 say? 🖤

hera

Oh, there is plenty I want 2 say. But nothing u want to 👂, trust me.

ephialtes

Sigh. 😔

Send

otis

Don't be sad, bro. You can run away w/ me & my beautiful  and it won't be weird at all!

ephialtes

If u say so. #ThirdWheel

🏹 Artemis

Check out my new look!

👍   REPLY

---

otis

Hey. Did u 👀 that creepy white deer?

ephialtes

Totally. Was just about 2 txt u the same thing!

Send

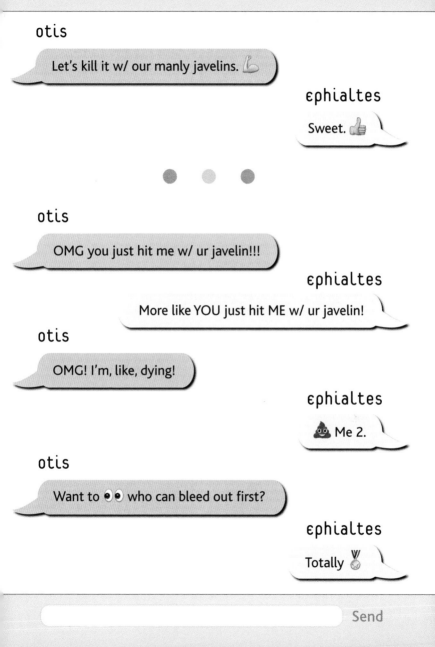

otis

I'm winni

ephialtes

No, I'm w

💪 GodBod 🦾

Otis now has pulse rate of 0 beats per minute.

Ephialtes now has pulse rate of 0 beats per minute.

Send

 Otis and Ephialtes have checked into Tartarus.

Artemis

Lol, can some1 pls tie them up w/ angry 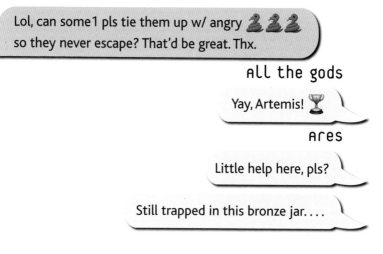 so they never escape? That'd be great. Thx.

All the gods

Yay, Artemis! 🏆

Ares

Little help here, pls?

Still trapped in this bronze jar. . . .

Send

- Orion -

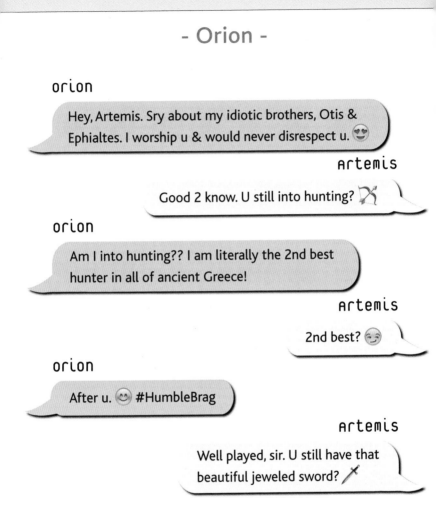

orion

Hey, Artemis. Sry about my idiotic brothers, Otis & Ephialtes. I worship u & would never disrespect u. 😍

Artemis

Good 2 know. U still into hunting? 🏹

orion

Am I into hunting?? I am literally the 2nd best hunter in all of ancient Greece!

Artemis

2nd best? 😏

orion

After u. 😊 #HumbleBrag

Artemis

Well played, sir. U still have that beautiful jeweled sword? 🗡

Send

orion

YOU MEAN THIS JEWELED SWORD?

Artemis

Lol, I wasn't sure what u were going 2 send me. 🙈

✅ Orion has checked into Island of Chios.

king of chios

How did u get here w/o a ⛵?

orion

NBD I can walk on water. #ForRealTho

king of chios

GTFO! That is so bad@$$! Can u also hunt? This island is covered in 🦁 🐯 and 🐻!

Send

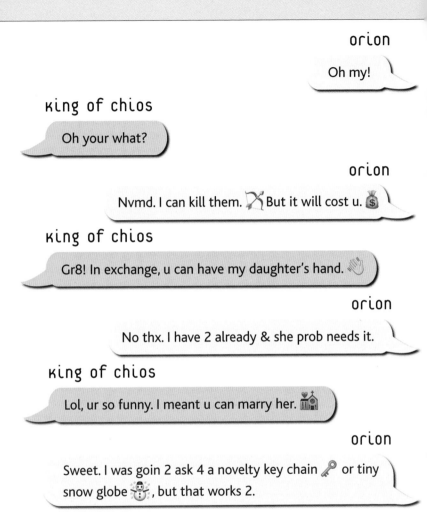

Orion

Killed all the 🦁 🐯 🐻 on the Island of Chios. #UrWelcome

👍 King Chios likes this.

[REPLY]

Princess of Chios: 😔

orion

So when can I marry ur daughter? 👫

king of chios

Um, about that . . .

orion

???

king of chios

I changed my mind. Also, there might still be 1 🦁 left bc I 👂 growling.

Send

orion

That is the sound of ur lies, King of Chios! I will kidnap the 👸 & run away w/ her . . . or at the very least ask her 2 dinner.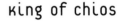

king of chios

Wait! Wait! Instead of getting 😡, let's just have a drink. 🍷

orion

That sounds like a trick  . . . but I am kinda thirsty. *Cheers*

● ● ●

king of chios

Keep refilling his 🍷 until he is 😵. Then blind him.

servant

● ● ●

Send

orion

> WTF?! Kng of Chios, u wil pay 4 ur treachery! I wil regain my  by staring in2 the ☼ —which I kno doesnt make sens at all but ⏰ me tryy!

> & dont even bothr writng back, bc I can't see ur msgs anywway. U jerk.

● ● ●

Hephaestus

> Oh no. What happened, Orion?

orion

> I can't 👀 ur txts, but if u happn 2 b Hephaestusss & r askng how u can help, send me a Cyclops 2 lead me 2 #TheRisingSun. ☼

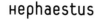
Hephaestus

> Consider it done. 👍

orion

> Again, IDK wut u wrote, but if u sed OK, thx.

Send

Hephaestus

Trust me. I know what it's like 2 have girl problems.

✅ Orion has checked into The Rising Sun.

orion

I can see again! 👀

King of chios

Oh 💩. G2g!

King of Chios

King of Chios has posted to the marketplace:
"Large, beautiful palace for sale by owner.
Motivated seller!"

👍   REPLY

Send

☑ Orion has checked into Empty Chios Palace.

orion

Well, that sux. The king is gone. How will I get my revenge?

Artemis

IDK. Want 2 go hunting 2gether all over the 🌍?

orion

Sure! 🏹

👨 Orion

Orion and Artemis have updated their status to: BEST friends.

👍   REPLY

Apollo: 😠

Send

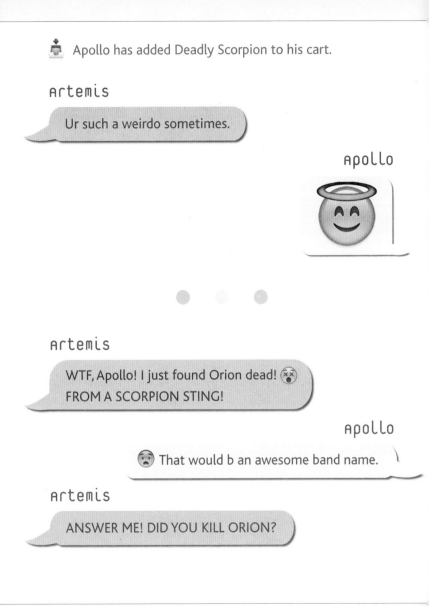

Apollo has added Deadly Scorpion to his cart.

Artemis

Ur such a weirdo sometimes.

Apollo

Artemis

WTF, Apollo! I just found Orion dead! 😵
FROM A SCORPION STING!

Apollo

😰 That would b an awesome band name.

Artemis

ANSWER ME! DID YOU KILL ORION?

Send

APOLLO

Sorry not sorry. He was getting way 2 close 2 u. 😠

ARTEMIS

Well, maybe I liked it, Apollo. Maybe 4 ONCE I liked having a relationship w/ a 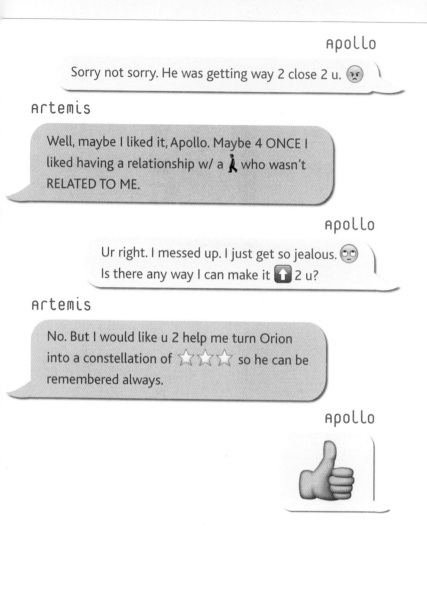 who wasn't RELATED TO ME.

APOLLO

Ur right. I messed up. I just get so jealous. 🙄 Is there any way I can make it ⬆️ 2 u?

ARTEMIS

No. But I would like u 2 help me turn Orion into a constellation of ☆☆☆ so he can be remembered always.

APOLLO

👍

Send

Artemis

Rest in peace, dear friend xo

Apollo likes this.

REPLY

Send

- Persephone -

Hades

Persephone, bae, wut's wrong?

Persephone

What do u mean, "What's wrong?" U kidnapped me and brought me 2 this godsforsaken underworld!!! It sucks here!! I want 2 go 🏠! 😠

Hades

CTFO! Every1 here worships you! Ur their queen!

Persephone

I don't want 2 b the 🧕 of the 💀. I want 2 b outside in the ☀️ and 💃 in forests.

Hades

Well, we have that 1 pomegranate 🌳. Why don't u have a pomegranate? It might cheer u up. 😬

Persephone

How many times do I have 2 tell u?! I'm not eating ur dead-people food! 🙅‍♀️

Send

persephone

Mom! I miss u! Come rescue me! #FOMO

Demeter

OMG, Persephone! I have been looking 4 u everywhere. Are u OK?

persephone

Yes, but I want 2 come 🏠. Hades abducted me when we were in the field that day and got separated. 😭

Demeter

I have been 😭 & the whole 🌍 has turned to ice and ❄️. I will not let anything bloom until I have u safely in my arms again. 🖤 I will find a way.

persephone

Pls hurry! I am getting rly hungry & my options r pretty limited down here. 😔

Demeter

Will do!

Send

zeus

Hey, Demeter. Can u pls let things bloom again? All the gods keep complaining that u've turned the 🌍 into some kind of icy wasteland and every1 is dying. 😵

Demeter

I'm not doing anything unless u help me get my daughter back from Hades.

Zeus has added Hermes to conversation.

zeus

Hermes, go down 2 Hades & see if u can talk some sense into Hades.

Hermes

OK, but just 2 b clear, the guy's name is Hades AND the place is called Hades?

zeus

Yeah. Just go w/ it.

Send

Group text: Hermes, Persephone, Hades

Hermes

Good news! I'm here 2 bring u 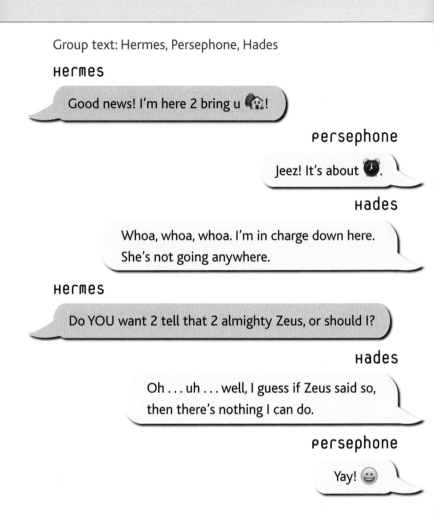!

Persephone

Jeez! It's about ⏰.

Hades

Whoa, whoa, whoa. I'm in charge down here.
She's not going anywhere.

Hermes

Do YOU want 2 tell that 2 almighty Zeus, or should I?

Hades

Oh . . . uh . . . well, I guess if Zeus said so,
then there's nothing I can do.

Persephone

Yay! 😀

Send

Hades

But there is one small issue.

Persephone

WHAT?

Hades

You ate some pomegranate seeds the other day. SoOoOo I guess u'll just have 2 stay 4ever. Because . . . arbitrary rules. LMAO

Persephone

That is bull💩! I had—at most—a handful of seeds, and it was an accident. I'm calling Zeus.

Hades

Good luck. The service sux down here.

Persephone

Just like everything else.

Send

Group text: Zeus, Demeter, Hades, Persephone

zeus

> WHAT NOW?! I'm trying to get some "me" time in w/ these 👯 b4 my wife gets back. 😏

Demeter

> Hades refuses to free Persephone even tho u commanded it! 😡

Hades

> Because she ate the food of the dead! U know the rules, Zeus.

Persephone

> I was tricked! He has been trying 2 get me 2 eat those damn pomegranate seeds ever since I got here!

zeus

> ENOUGH. Let's agree 2 a compromise, shall we? From now on, Persephone will spend 1/2 the year w/ her mother aboveground, and the other 1/2 belowground in Hades. Then everyone's 😄, right?

Send

Demeter

No way! I refuse to bring warmth and ☀ and 🐝 for any amt of time my daughter and I are apart. 😔 💔

zeus

So be it. We'll have 6 mos of warmth ☀ and 6 mos of cold. ⛄

persephone

So unfair. But I'm just glad to b back w/ u again, Mom.

zeus

So, Demeter. In the off-season . . .

persephone

Don't even think about it, Zeus.

zeus

Can't blame a guy for trying. 😉

Send

- King Midas -

servant

> King Midas, we found this satyr 😴 in ur favorite garden. 🌹🌹🌹

king midas

> I guess that's y they call it a flower BED. 😂

servant

> 🙄 Lol, good one. So wut should we do w/ him? Cut him up into tiny bits? 🎉

king midas

> Nah, let him go. He's harmless.

servant

king midas

😄

Send

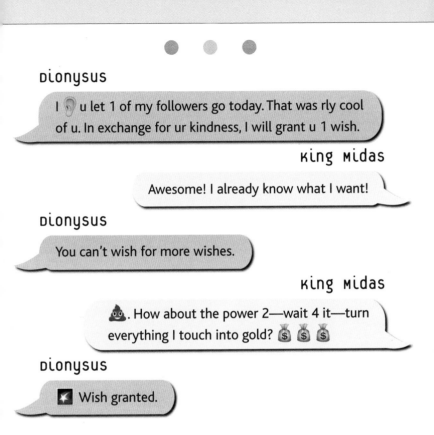

King Midas

My wish came true! Everything I touch turns 2 gold! Even my 🖥️ and 📱. Man, gold is hard 2 type on. NBD, if anyone needs me, I'll just be over here in my golden chair, sitting at my golden table, eating my solid gold food 🍗 and drinking solid gold drinks 🍺 from my gold chalice. Oh 💩. Didn't think of that.

👍   REPLY

Princess Marigold: Oh no, Daddy! 🙊 You're going 2 die of hunger and thirst! 😵

King Midas: OMG, ur right. Come here & give me a hug b4 I die. 😭

Princess Marigold: OTW!

King Midas: Oh 💩. Now my poor daughter has turned 2 gold! FML.

King Midas

> Dionysus, this 💩 is not cool.

Dionysus

> Okay, okay. I will reverse the spell. Go 2 the river Pactolus 💧 & the water will fix everything.

Send

King Midas

I will do that rite now. THANKS! 👜

Dionysus

Did u learn ur lesson? 📝

King Midas

Yes! Nxt time I will just have trespassers cut up in2 tiny pieces! ✂️

Dionysus

LOL

Send

- Echo -

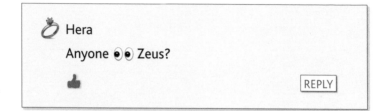

Hera

Anyone 👀 Zeus?

👍 REPLY

zeus

Echo, can u distract Hera while I sneak away? 🏃 I don't want her 2 know I've been messing around w/ other 👯.

echo

K. Want me 2 just talk 2 her incessantly?

zeus

● ● ●

Send

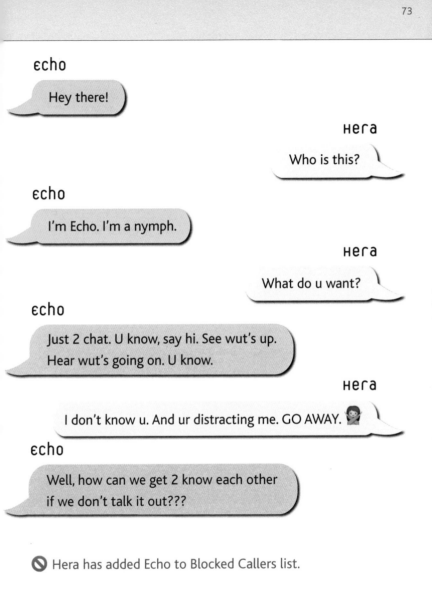

zeus

Escaped! Thx 4 distracting Hera. Ur awesome, Echo.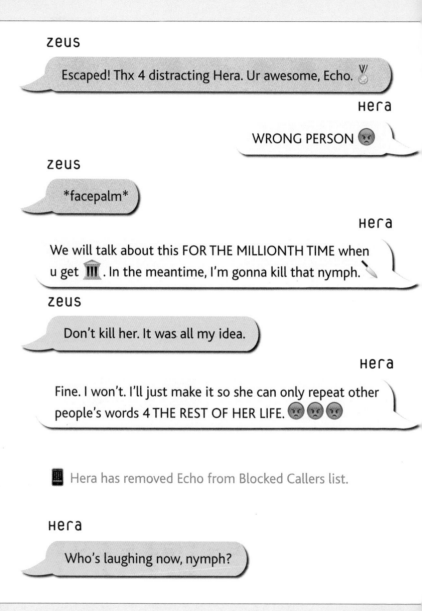

Hera

WRONG PERSON 😡

zeus

facepalm

Hera

We will talk about this FOR THE MILLIONTH TIME when u get 🏛. In the meantime, I'm gonna kill that nymph. 🔪

zeus

Don't kill her. It was all my idea.

Hera

Fine. I won't. I'll just make it so she can only repeat other people's words 4 THE REST OF HER LIFE. 😡😡😡

📱 Hera has removed Echo from Blocked Callers list.

Hera

Who's laughing now, nymph?

Send

- Narcissus -

Narcissus

Narcissus has added "Myself" to his interests.

👍

REPLY

Echo

Echo has added "Narcissus" to her interests.

👍 Narcissus likes this.

REPLY

Narcissus

Just saw the most beautiful 👶 on 🌍. In a pool of water. 💧 I'm in love. 💚 I can't eat. ❌ 🍵 I can't drink. ❌ 🍹 I can't sleep. ❌ 😴 All I can do is 👀 into this magical reflective surface just inches from my face. This person (who actually looks a lot like me, except more watery) is perfect in every way. I would rather die than look away. 🙈

👍

REPLY

Send

🧕 Echo

> 👨 Narcissus
>
> Just saw the most beautiful 👨 on 🌍. In a pool of water. 😍 I'm in love. 💔 I can't eat. ❌ 🍽️ I can't drink. ❌ 🍹 I can't sleep. ❌ 😴 All I can do is 👀 into this magical reflective surface just inches from my face. This person (who actually looks a lot like me, except more watery) is perfect in every way. I would rather die than look away. 🙍
>
> 👍   REPLY

👍   REPLY

Hermes: Famous last words, Echo. Guess it's time for me to bring you and Narcissus to the underworld. 💀 💀

Send

- Medusa and Perseus -

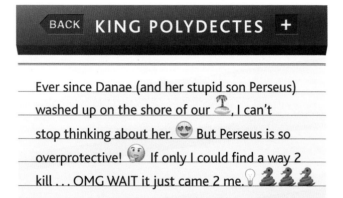

‹BACK KING POLYDECTES +

Ever since Danae (and her stupid son Perseus) washed up on the shore of our 🏝️, I can't stop thinking about her. 😍 But Perseus is so overprotective! 🤔 If only I could find a way 2 kill . . . OMG WAIT it just came 2 me. 💡 🐍 🐍 🐍

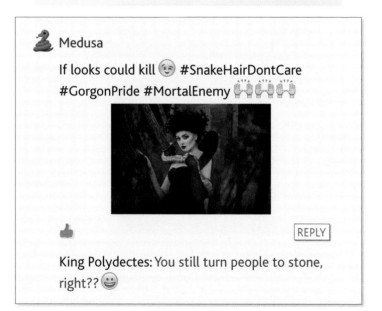

🐍 Medusa

If looks could kill 😜 #SnakeHairDontCare
#GorgonPride #MortalEnemy 🖕🖕🖕🖕🖕

👍   REPLY

King Polydectes: You still turn people to stone, right?? 😀

Send

King Polydectes

Hey, Perseus. I have a task that is so special, you are the only person in the 🌍 who can do it. 🏆 🥈 ⭐

Perseus

If it's going on a double date w/ u and my mom, the answer is still NO.

King Polydectes

Lol, no, no. What I want now is much less creepy. (Ha.) I want u to behead Medusa.

Perseus

THE Medusa? R u serious?

King Polydectes

Yeah. #LongStory

Perseus

But u know if u look @ her directly, ur immediately turned 2 stone, right?

King Polydectes

Lol yeah. That's why I'm sending YOU. 😇 haha jk jk

Send

Perseus

www.GoSendMeDrachmas-PerseusFund.com

FML. The king wants me to behead Medusa. Little help here?

👍 REPLY

Hermes: I have a pair of winged sandals you can borrow.

Perseus: Uhh, thx, dude. I was thinking more like weapons, tho.

Hephaestus: Got it. I'll send u a 🗡 ASAP.

Athena: And I can get u a mirrored shield. 🛡

Hades: My helmet of invisibility is here somewhere. . . .

Perseus: Hell yeah!

Hades: But I have to find it first. 🙁

Send

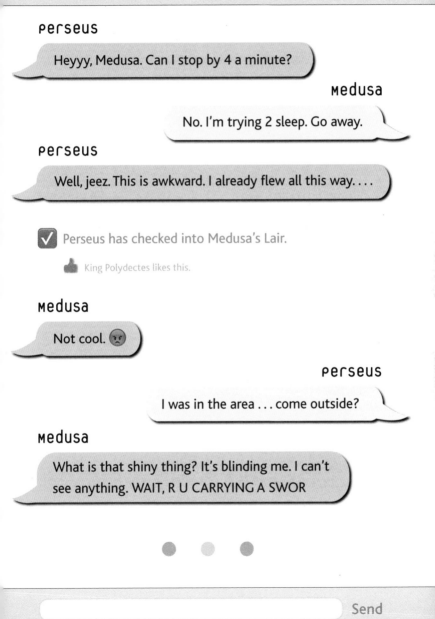

perseus

It is done.

king polydectes

OMG rly!??!

perseus

Yah, I used the mirror 2 see her w/o getting petrified. Then I cut off her head. I'd send a pic but . . . it isn't pretty. . . .

king polydectes

Wow. Did NOT see that coming.

perseus

Neither did she lol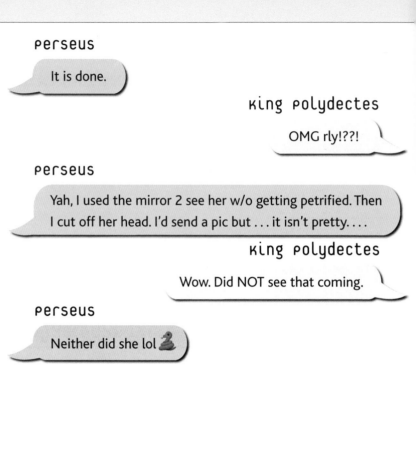

Send

- Tantalus and Pelops -
(or How the Olympics Came to Be)

Tantalus

Tantalus has created an event:
Enormous Dinner Party @ My Place.

👍 Olympian Gods like this.

REPLY

BACK **TANTALUS** +

I want 2 serve the best food possible . . .
🍎🧀🧀🍖 . . . but nothing seems good
enough 4 my guests. Hmm. 🤔 Maybe my
perfect son, Pelops, will have a suggestion. . . .
Wait a second—BETTER IDEA! 💡 I'll make my
PERFECT son into the PERFECT dish! 🔪 Why
didn't I think of this earlier? I'll miss him, sure,
but this party will go down in history!
🎉 FTW!

Send

84

 Tantalus

Tonight I'll be serving a new dish: Pelops Stew.

👃 ✋ 👀 🍲

👍   REPLY

Hermes: That's what I call a family recipe lol.

Olympian Gods: WTF?! That is so gross. 😷

Tantalus: Why is every1 freaking out? I thought u guys 🤍 human sacrifice???

Olympian Gods: We HATE human sacrifice.
🙈 🙉 🙊 Duh. So now we have no choice but 2 banish u 2 the underworld 🔥 & bring ur son back 2 life. 🙋

Send

Pelops

Ugh. I don't feel so good. Wut happened? And why am I missing a piece of my shoulder??

👍   REPLY

Olympian Gods: HERMES!
Hermes: *Shrugs* I was hungry.
Olympian Gods: Here, take this piece of ivory & use it 2 replace the missing bone.
Pelops: Do I need 2 worry about poachers? 🐼
Poseidon: Here, take this fleet of fast 🐎🐎🐎 and u can escape ur past & start a new life.
Pelops: OK, thanks!

pelops

Hey, girl.

Hippodamia

Hi.

king oenomaus

Don't talk 2 my daughter! She is the PRINCESS, for 😢 out loud! 👸

Send

Hippodamia

Sry, my dad just got this app that sends him duplicates of all my txts. FML. He's a little overprotective. 😊

Pelops

Seems that way. Couldn't help but notice the 12 💀s hanging by ur front gate.

Hippodamia

#SingleBecause

Pelops

Lol, he doesn't 🙀 me. Can I take u out sometime?

King Oenomaus

The only way u can take her out is if u beat me in a chariot race. 🐎

Pelops

That doesn't sound so bad.

Hippodamia

Well, he strategically 4got 2 mention that his 🐎s r the fastest 🐎s on 🌍.

Send

King Oenomaus

And if u lose, I get 2 add ur 💀 2 my collection.

Pelops

Normally, I would just move on 2 a less dangerous gf, but I don't rly have anywhere else 2 go rite now, so  it—I'm down. #YOLO

King Oenomaus

King Oenomaus has created an event:
Chariot Race: Me vs. Pelops.

👍 REPLY

Hermes: Side bets! Place ur side bets here! 💰

Hippodamia

I need u.

stable boy

OMG, I need u 2. Want 2 run away 2gether?

Send

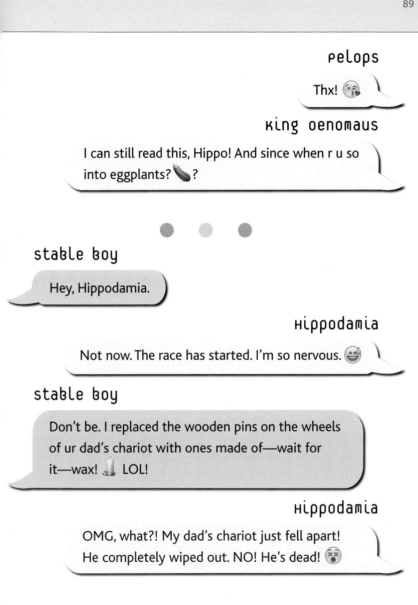

pelops

I won! Yay! OMG! Your dad! No! So many things @ once!

Hippodamia

U'll never guess what just happened.

stable boy

Hey, Hippodamia.

Hippodamia

Not now. The race has started. I'm so nervous. 😓

stable boy

Don't be. I replaced the wooden pins on the wheels of ur dad's chariot with ones made of---wait for it---wax! ⬇️ LOL!

Hippodamia

OMG, what?! My dad's chariot just fell apart! He completely wiped out. NO! He's dead! 😵

pelops

WHAT?! I can't believe it. Throw that stable boy into the 🌊. (Even tho he basically saved my life.)

Send

 Pelops and Hippodamia have added "Wedding Rings: Certified Midas Gold!" to their cart.

Pelops

Now that I am the new 👑, I would like 2 host a grand feast 🍗 🍷 🍗 🍷 🥒 in honor of my late father-in-law, along w/ an athletic competition of strength 🏋️, endurance 🚣, and speed 🏃 in Olympia. #TheOlympics 🏅 👍

REPLY

Hermes: Sweet. How often?

Pelops: What do u mean? It's a 1-shot deal.

Hermes: I made bank off the last race. 💰 💰 💰 Could u make this a recurring thing?

Pelops: Fine. How about every 5 yrs?

Hermes: I was thinking 3. 😇

Pelops: Sigh. Let's meet halfway. Every 4 yrs.

Hermes: 👍

Send

- Oedipus -

oracle of Delphi

FYI, I had a prophecy 🔮 this morning that ur son will 🗡️ u 😵 & marry ur 👰, Jocasta. Just thought u should know.

King Laius

😱 STFU! R u sure it wasn't food poisoning from leftover Pelops Stew? 🍲 🤢

oracle of Delphi

I have literally nvr been wrong about anything in my entire life.

King Laius

💩 FML

● ● ●

King Laius

Hey, you work for me, right? Can u do me a favor? I need u 2 bring my son, Oedipus, out into the 🌲🌲🌲 & kill him. 🗡️ 😭

Send

servant

Ur newborn 👶? WTF?!

King Laius

Do it. Or else I'll kill u instead.

☑ Servant and Oedipus have checked into Deep, Dark Forest in Corinth.

🍴 **Servant**
I'm not a baby killer. And this is creepy AF. I'm getting out of here! 🏃

👍   REPLY

☑ Corinthian Shepherd has checked into Deep, Dark Forest in Corinth.

🐑 **Corinthian Shepherd**
Found this newborn 👶 in the woods! 🌲 🌲 🌲 Any1 interested?

👍 King and Queen of Corinth like this.   REPLY

Queen of Corinth: Yay! 🎉 Pls bring the 👶 to our 🏠 & we will raise him as our own. 👪

Send

oracle of Delphi

FYI, u r destined 2 kill ur father 🗡️ & marry ur mother. 👰 Just thought u should know, now that u r all grown 🔼 & everything.

oedipus

OMG, what?! Do u have the wrong guy??? My name is actually pronounced w/o the 1st "O" so ppl mix me up w/ Edipus from the next town over. 👬

oracle of Delphi

YES. YOU. You'll kill ur dad and marry ur mom.

oedipus

💩 The King and Queen of Corinth?! Say it ain't so! I 🖤 my parents so much! I must run away & never come back. 🏃

Send

King Laius

Out for a stroll in the . I'll be gone for a while. I take my strolls very srsly. Nobody better try to get in the way of my STROLL!!! ⚔️

Jocasta

Lol, you and your strolls!

😂

BACK **OEDIPUS** +

Just got in2 the biggest fight w/ these jerks trying 2 push me off the  path on my way 2 Thebes. It turned in2 an all-out brawl & I ended up killing all but 1 guy!!! One of them was wearing a crown. Which IMHO is kind of weird for just a normal guy out on a stroll. #SelfDefense #QuestionMark

Send

 The Sphinx has checked into City Wall Outside Thebes.

 Oedipus has checked into City Wall Outside Thebes.

Send

тhe sphinx

What r u looking @? Haven't u ever seen an enormous winged monster with a female head + a lion's body b4? 👩 🦁

oedipus

Can't say that I have.

тhe sphinx

Well, get outta here. I am vry obviously guarding this gate & eating any1 who tries 2 go in or out!!!

oedipus

Well, I want 2 get thru.

тhe sphinx

The only way u can get thru is if u can answer my riddle: What walks on 4 feet in the morning, 2 feet at noon, and 3 feet in the evening? 👟 👟

oedipus

I know. It's a person! As a child, we crawl on 4 legs. As an adult, we walk on 2 feet. And when we're old, we often walk w/ a cane.

Send

The sphinx

NOOOOOO!!!!! U r correct & I have therefore lost all my powers. There is nothing 4 me 2 do now except plummet 2 a violent death. 😭

oedipus

And there is nothing 4 me 2 do now except be welcomed as a hero 💪 & marry ur beautiful and conveniently newly widowed queen, Jocasta. 👰🤵 💒

👸 Queen Jocasta

Oedipus's and my Save-the-Dates have arrived! Love you, baby xoxo

👍 Oracle of Delphi likes this.

REPLY

Oedipus: Love you more. #HotMama

Hermes: I love a good family affair.

Send

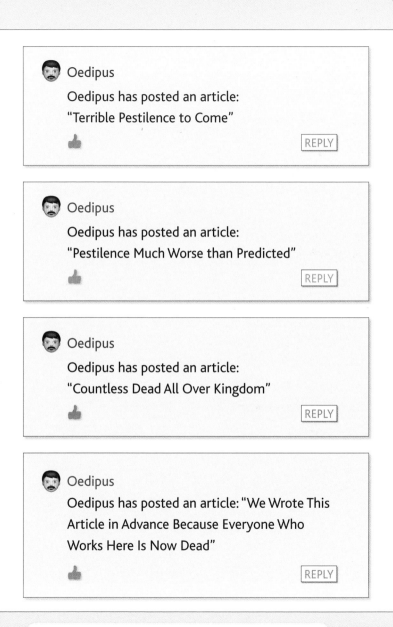

Oedipus

Oedipus has posted an article:
"Terrible Pestilence to Come"

👍 REPLY

Oedipus

Oedipus has posted an article:
"Pestilence Much Worse than Predicted"

👍 REPLY

Oedipus

Oedipus has posted an article:
"Countless Dead All Over Kingdom"

👍 REPLY

Oedipus

Oedipus has posted an article: "We Wrote This
Article in Advance Because Everyone Who
Works Here Is Now Dead"

👍 REPLY

Send

Oedipus

Oh, man! I still had 6 months left on my subscription. 😞

👍 | REPLY

Seer: If u want 2 put an end 2 the pestilence, u need 2 avenge the death of the last king. 👑
Oedipus: I will! I will find his murderer & put out both his 👀. Guards! Find out who did this!

🔍 HermesList 🔍

WANTED: If anyone has information involving King Laius's murder, please notify local authorities immediately. Information leading to the arrest and conviction of his murderer will result in a 10,000 drachma reward.

REPLY

Do NOT contact us with unsolicited services or offers.
Posted by Oedipus

Servant: I was w/ King Laius when he was waylaid on his 🏔 stroll.
Oedipus: Tell me who killed him. 🗡

Send

Servant: Promise not to get mad?

Oedipus: Yeah. Just say it.

Servant: Okay. It was you. ⚔️

Oedipus: WTF?!

Servant: Also, I was the one who left you in the 🌲 🌲 🌲 as a 👶, and I saw the King and Queen of Corinth take you in. I was going to tell u the truth about ur past, but I guess I just never got around to it. 😬

Oedipus: FML

jocasta

Oedipus, r the rumors true? That ur rly my long-lost son???

oedipus

I don't know how to tell u this . . . but yes. 😬

Mom?

Hellooo?

Send

- Prometheus -

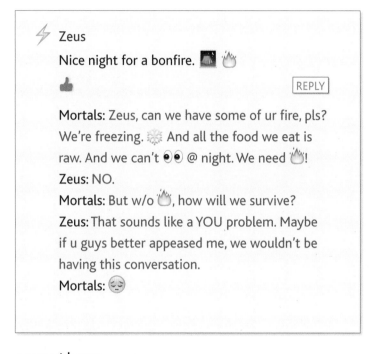

⚡ Zeus

Nice night for a bonfire. 🏞️ 🔥

👍 [REPLY]

Mortals: Zeus, can we have some of ur fire, pls? We're freezing. ❄️ And all the food we eat is raw. And we can't 👀 @ night. We need 🔥!

Zeus: NO.

Mortals: But w/o 🔥, how will we survive?

Zeus: That sounds like a YOU problem. Maybe if u guys better appeased me, we wouldn't be having this conversation.

Mortals: 😔

prometheus

Psst. Mortals. I feel ur pain.

mortals

Rly?

Send

prometheus

Yes. I'm going 2 steal 1 of Zeus's ⚡s so u can have 🔥 on 🌍.

mortals

OMG, we would 🖤 u 4everrr. 💞

prometheus

Np

⚡ **Zeus**

Hmm. My bag of ⚡s seems kind of light today.

👍 REPLY

Hermes: Isn't a bag of ⚡ always LIGHT, Zeus? Lol

Zeus: 😂 Oh, Hermes. U slay me.

Hermes: More like u slay every1 else! 😏

Zeus: Bwahaha! But really, WHO STOLE MY LIGHTNING BOLTS?!?!

Hermes: IDK, but I saw on my feed this a.m. that humans have 🔥 again. Coincidence?

Send

Hermes

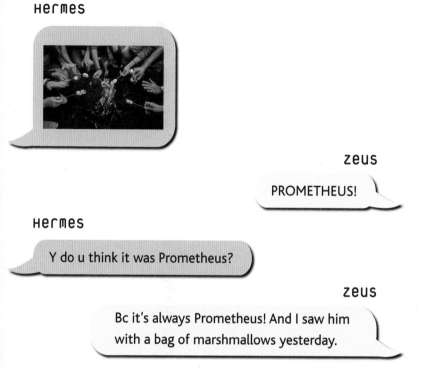

zeus

PROMETHEUS!

Hermes

Y do u think it was Prometheus?

zeus

Bc it's always Prometheus! And I saw him with a bag of marshmallows yesterday.

Send

Prometheus

FML. Zeus found out I stole 🔥 4 the humans & chained me 2 a giant rock overlooking the 🌊 4ever.

👍 REPLY

Zeus: Just wait till sunrise. ☁️
Prometheus: What happens @ 🌅 ?
Zeus: An eagle will come & eat ur liver.
Prometheus: Well, that sux. But I guess I can get over it, if it's just the 1 time.
Zeus: Bwahaha! OR I can magically make ur liver regrow every night so this happens every single day.
Prometheus: Meh. That seems unnecessary.
Hercules: Don't lose hope, Prometheus! I'll rescue u!
Prometheus: Yeah???
Hercules: Yeah, but not for approx. 1,000 yrs. ⏳
Prometheus: 😭

Send

- Daedalus and Icarus -

ıcarus

Dad, I'm bored. 😕

ᴅaeᴅalus

Of course ur bored. We're being held prisoner by King Minos bc I helped Theseus figure out the solution 2 the labyrinth before the Minotaur could eat him! 👿

ıcarus

How DID he get out of that maze alive? The 🌎 may never know. 😏

ᴅaeᴅalus

It's common sense! He used a ball of thread, unwinding as he went, so that once he killed the giant beast, he could follow the thread back to his starting place.

ıcarus

WHOA, I just assumed GPS or something. Thread would take 4ever.

Speaking of which . . . when are we getting out of here? ⏳

Send

Daedalus

It's been like 10 minutes. But relax. I have an idea.

Icarus

The last time u had an idea, we ended up in here!

Daedalus

No. This is different. I'm making wings out of wax and feathers. If we wear them on our backs we should b able 2 fly out of a window & escape.

Icarus

WTG, Dad!

Daedalus

Just don't fly 2 close 2 the ☀ or the wax will melt & u will plunge hundreds of feet to a terrible, horrible death.

Icarus

Yeah, yeah, yeah. Whatever.

✅ Daedalus and Icarus have checked into Highest Tower in Castle.

Send

Icarus

#FinalSelfie

✅ Icarus has checked into Davy Jones's Locker.

✅ Daedalus has checked into Sicily.

> **King of Sicily:** Sorry about ur son. But wut u did was super cool. And u can live here now & do awesome renovations 2 my like u did 4 King Minos. 👑
> **Daedalus:** 👍
> **King Minos:** King of Sicily, I know u r harboring Daedalus! He is mine. Give him back. 😠
> **King of Sicily:** IDK wut u r talking about. 😇
> **King Minos:** I know u have him. ICYMI he literally posted a earlier in this thread. U just wait. I will find a way 2 get him back.

Send

King Minos

King Minos has posted a challenge: Whoever can get a thin thread thru this conch shell will be rewarded w/ lavish gifts. 🐚 💰 💍 🎁

👍   REPLY

King of Sicily: Ooh! I 🖤 challenges. And lavish gifts. Daedalus, how can I get a thread all the way through this twisty, turny 🐚?
Daedalus: If u tie a thread 2 an 🐜 and put 🛢 at the other end, it will crawl through, pulling the thread the whole way.
King of Sicily: Brilliant!
King Minos: Aha! I knew u had Daedalus. Give him back!
King of Sicily: OK, OK. U caught me. Why don't u come here & get him yourself? I'll even throw a huge feast in your honor. 🍖 🍺

Send

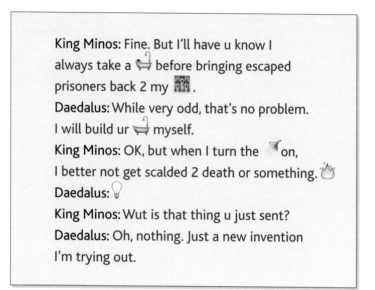

King Minos: Fine. But I'll have u know I always take a 🛁 before bringing escaped prisoners back 2 my 🏰.

Daedalus: While very odd, that's no problem. I will build ur 🛁 myself.

King Minos: OK, but when I turn the 🚿 on, I better not get scalded 2 death or something. 🔥

Daedalus: 💡

King Minos: Wut is that thing u just sent?

Daedalus: Oh, nothing. Just a new invention I'm trying out.

✅ King Minos has checked into Sicily.

✅ King Minos has checked into Daedalus's Special Bathtub.

👴 King Minos
AHHHHHHHHHH!!!!!!!!!!!!!! I'm burning to death!!!!!!! I can't believe u did the thing I explicitly asked u NOT to do, Daedalus!!!!!!

👍 People of Crete like this.   REPLY

Send

Daedalus

#Blessed

👍 King of Sicily likes this.

REPLY

King of Sicily: #TypicalDaedalus

Send

The 411 for Those Not in the Know

411: Information

4EVER: Forever

AF: As F*ck

AMT: Amount

B4: Before

BAE: Babe

BFF: Best Friends Forever

BTW: By The Way

CTFO: Chill The F*ck Out

FML: F*ck My Life

FOMO: Fear Of Missing Out

FTW: For The Win

G2G: Got To Go

GTFO: Get The F*ck Out

HMU: Hit Me Up

ICYMI: In Case You Missed It

IDK: I Don't Know

IMHO: In My Humble Opinion

JIC: Just In Case

JK: Just Kidding

LMAO: Laughing My A$$ Off

LOL: Laughing Out Loud

MOS: Months

Send

MSGS: Messages

MTB: Meant To Be

NBD: No Big Deal

NP: No Problem

NTM: Not Too Much

NVMD: Never Mind

NXT: Next

OMG: Oh My God

OTP: One True Pairing

OTW: On The Way

PLS: Please

PPL: People

RLY: Really

ROTFLMAO: Rolling On The Floor Laughing My A$$ Off

SMH: Shaking My Head

SRSLY: Seriously

STFU: Shut The F*ck Up

SUX: Sucks

TBH: To Be Honest

THX: Thanks

TL;DR: Too Long; Didn't Read

TXT: Text

UR: Your or You Are

VRY: Very

WTF: What The F*ck?

WTG: Way To Go

WUT: What

YOLO: You Only Live Once

Send

some emotions you might find in this book

😍 Affectionate

😠 Angry

😅 Anxious

🙁 Confusion

😎 Cool

😵 Dead (or Dying)

😞 Disappointed

😳 Embarrassed (and/or Drunk)

😘 Flirty

😉 Friendly (wink, wink)

😜 Goofy

🙂 Happy

😇 Innocent

😐 Nothing

😡 Really Angry

Really Happy

Rolling Eyes

Sad

Sad (and Crying)

Sad (and Sobbing)

Scared (and Screaming)

Sheepish (and/or Grimacing)

Shocked

Sick

Sleepy

Sly

Tears of Joy

Thinking

Unamused

Warm Fuzzies

Send

COURTNEY CARBONE studied English and creative writing in the US and Australia before becoming a children's book writer and editor in New York City. Her favorite things include Brit lit, trivia nights, board games, stand-up comedy, improv, bookstores, libraries, brick-oven pizza, salted-caramel macarons, theme parties, sharks, puns, portmanteaus, and '90s pop culture. 😎

@CBCarbone
CourtneyCarbone.com

Send